PUFFIN BOO

Editor: Kaye V

Robin's Real Engine and other Stories

William Mayne is a writer with a special way of seeing things, of noticing quite ordinary everyday oddments about the way people talk and do things and making them seem special and interesting enough to think about. Usually he writes for older children of about ten to twelve, but here collected together in one book for the very first time are three stories he has written for readers of about six upwards. They are simpler and shorter than his other books, but all of them have their proper share of the unforgettable William Mayne 'seeing magic'.

Robin's Real Engine tells the story of Robin, whose three big sisters saw a steam engine go by while he was in the bath – or did they? It will be particularly enjoyed by any children who come at the tail end of the family.

The Big Egg is a simple story with big thoughts in it, telling how Katharine found a huge blue egg in the hedge, and liked it so much that it felt like part of her. 'It's a Katharine egg,' she said. 'I laid it.' It was a good pretend, but what the children did with the egg after they took it back home to Daddy was pretty good too.

The Toffee Join is a delightful wet-day story in which five cousins set out on a mystery visit to their Granny, each of them on her instructions carrying a bit of sugar, or butter, or syrup – though what they arrive with is a different matter.

WILLIAM MAYNE

Robin's Real Engine and other Stories

PUFFIN BOOKS

in association with Hamish Hamilton Children's Books

Puffin Books, Penguin Books Ltd, Harmondsworth, Middlesex, England
Penguin Books, 625 Madison Avenue, New York, New York 10022, U.S.A.
Penguin Books Australia Ltd, Ringwood, Victoria, Australia
Penguin Books Canada Ltd, 41 Steelcase Road West, Markham, Ontario, Canada
Penguin Books (N.Z.) Ltd, 182–190 Wairau Road, Auckland 10, New Zealand

—

Robin's Real Engine first published by Hamish Hamilton 1972
The Big Egg first published by Hamish Hamilton 1967
The Toffee Join first published by Hamish Hamilton 1968
Published in one volume in Puffin Books 1975
Reprinted 1977

—

Made and printed in Great Britain by
Cox & Wyman Ltd, London, Reading and Fakenham
Set in Monotype Times

CONTENTS

Robin's Real Engine

Illustrated by

Mary Dinsdale

The girls had been lying on the hall floor for a long time, reading and drawing. They were all separated out, Biddy in one place,

Lucy in another,

and Kate near the clock,

but they were near enough to each other to kick anybody they wanted, which is what they did sometimes, or to prod the backs of each others' knees with a sharp pencil, which they did at other times, or to tie Lucy's hair round a chair leg, which Biddy did once. Lucy thought it was quite funny, and began to save up something even funnier to do to Biddy, like making the clock strike eight midnights at her straight off, all haunted and black.

But you can't be sure of clocks, she thought, and it might ring out just a small afternoon time, and that would be no use at all, even on the most ticklish person.

The day had already come through all the afternoon, and got past tea-time, and midnight was still to come, half a clock away.

Then Robin came in from the playroom. He and Mummy were beginning the game called Putting Robin to Bed. Robin jumped on Biddy.

'I'm a dog,' he said. 'Black dog. I am going to eat you. There, Biddy, I have eaten you.'

'I like it,' said Biddy. 'Eat me again.' So Robin ate her again. Then he went to Lucy.

'I shall eat you,' he said.

'I shall eat *you*,' said Lucy, showing her teeth.

'No you shallent,' said Robin, and he crawled over her and ate her up.

'That was dreadful,' said Lucy. So Robin ate her again.

Mummy came to watch. 'What a big supper, Robin.'

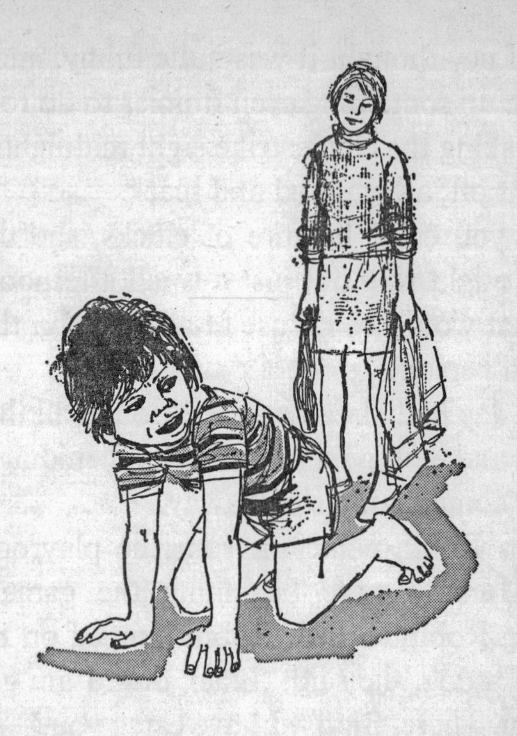

'He isn't here,' said Robin. 'I am a black dog.'

'I expect you belong to Robin,' said Mummy.

'No,' said the black dog. 'I belong to me. Kate, I am going to eat you up. Two times.'

But Kate understood about Robin, and she ate him up once, and twice, and a whole third time.

'That was lovely, Kate,' he said. 'Do it again.'

'I'm full up to my back legs,' said Kate.

'Back teeth,' said Mummy.

'Now I'm one of those things,' said Robin,

lying on his back and waving his arms and legs.

'Robin,' said Kate, 'you can't do that. I haven't spat you out.'

Robin waited until he was spat out, and then he was one of those things.

'I know, I was telling you about them,' said Mummy. 'We'll see them tomorrow if it doesn't rain too much. A steam engine. There'll be steam engines at Oxford Fair and we'll see them working the roundabouts and swing boats. When I was a little girl . . .'

'Like Kate,' said Lucy, because Kate was the littlest girl.

'Like Kate,' said Mummy, and Lucy was pleased not to be a little girl. 'And when I was a middle girl like Lucy, and when I was a bit bigger like Biddy, I used to see steam engines on the road. They were called traction engines, and they smelt like fires and they sounded like machines and they had big wheels and smoke and men driving them and they were hot and black.'

'Robin's just like one,' said Biddy.

'Yes,' said Mummy. 'And they had to get water from ponds and troughs and even from taps in houses. Now girls, it's stopped raining. You can go outside for a little while, because Robin and I

have to go and see about a tap and some water. Go on, you don't need your coats.'

'Robin went outside, to a pond,' said the steam engine, lying on its back and turning all its wheels round very fast.

'Steam engines are just as good,' said Mummy. 'Who's going to be the driver of this one?'

The steam engine thought about it while Mummy picked up pencils and papers and one of Kate's socks from the hall floor, and put them all down again in slightly different places. She called it tidying up.

Robin decided that Mummy was to be the

driver and that she had to carry him. She picked him up. 'Hot and black,' she said.

'And I'm a dog as well,' he said.

'All those things,' said Mummy. She went to the front door and opened it.

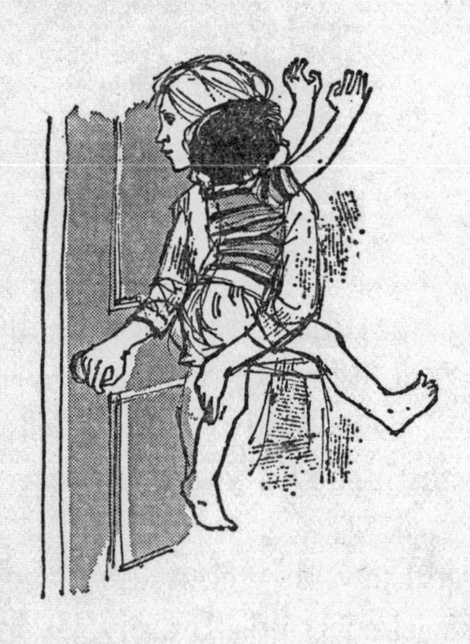

'We don't go this way,' said Robin.

'I know,' said Mummy. 'But I can hear those girls breaking the windows any minute now. Biddy,' she shouted, when she had the door open, 'stop it.'

'What?' said Biddy, coming round the corner of the house. 'I mean, I heard what you said, but what did you mean?'

'Stotting that ball against the house,' said Mummy. 'You'll break a window.'

'Stotting,' said Biddy. 'What's that? I never heard of stotting. Did you ever hear of stotting, Lucy?'

'No,' said Lucy. 'Is it something wicked?'

'Nearly wicked,' said Mummy. 'It's what I used to say when I was a little girl.'

'As old as who?' said Biddy.

'As old as everybody,' said Mummy. 'Stotting means bouncing a ball, and you're not to do it against the house. There's all the rest of England out here, so go and play in that but don't go out of the garden or the yard or up the lane to the road.'

‘Stotting,’ said Biddy. ‘We never heard of that. I think they’re animals, stottings, like goats.’

‘And they catch you,’ said Lucy, turning into one just as Robin had turned into a dog and a steam engine. Lucy caught Kate, and Kate turned into an even bigger stotting and caught Biddy.

Mummy went in and closed the door against them. One of the girls, but nobody knows which one, stotted the ball against the front door once, and then all three of them ran off to play somewhere else.

The steam engine driver carried the steam

engine upstairs. She looked out of the landing window. 'Kate's left her sock behind,' she said. But Robin did not care.

It took Mummy a long time to get him into the bath. She found that steam engines get undressed in a different way from dogs and boys. Steam engines have such big wheels that it is very hard to get their jumpers off. Black dogs have their vests taken off downwards instead of upwards. Boys have to wear Biddy's bath hat and use Daddy's blue soap.

Robin discovered that steam engines can lift up

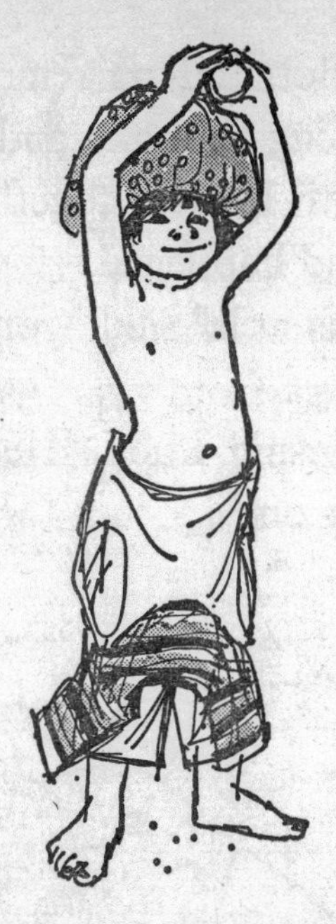

their right leg and bang it down again very hard so that there is a big splash. He found that the left leg made a better splash because it splashed Mummy. His hat fell off.

Biddy came running into the bathroom. Lucy was just behind her and Kate came shouting up the stairs. Robin thought he would make the biggest splash of all and lifted up both his legs together and fell over backwards and went under the water.

'There now,' said Mummy to Biddy, 'you've drowned him.' Robin did not mind being drowned.

He spluttered a lot, but he remembered the big splash he was going to make and he made it; he banged down both his legs together and then sat up to see what had happened.

'I'm drowned as well,' said Mummy, drying her face.

'Look at him,' said Lucy. 'He's sitting in the bath with nothing on.'

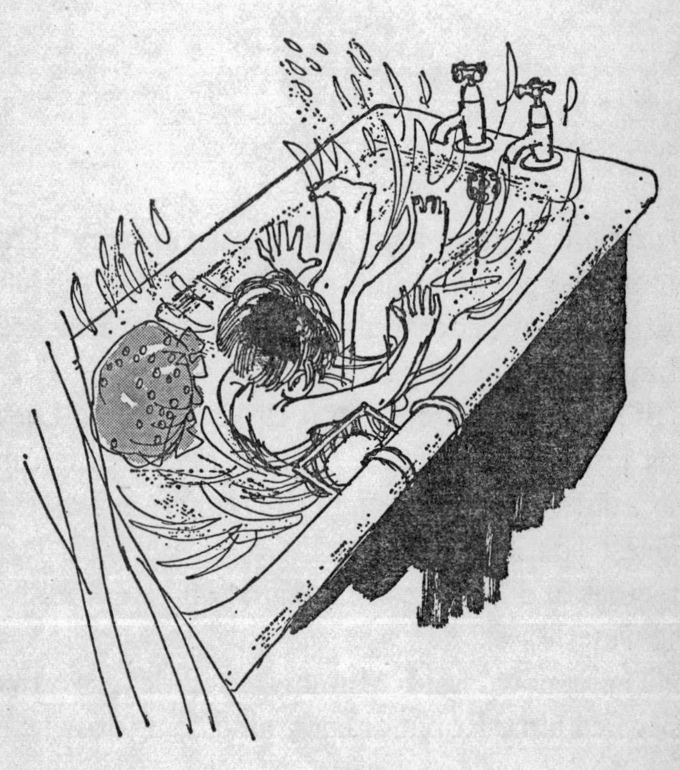

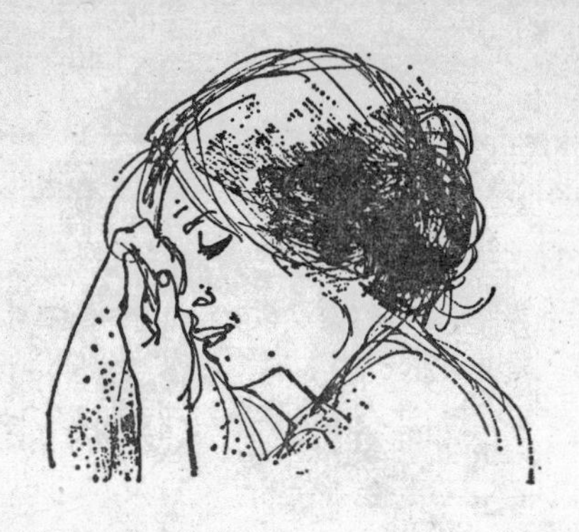

'Just like a boy,' said Biddy.

'Who's next?' said Kate. 'Why is it always my turn?'

'Everybody's next,' said Mummy. 'So stay where you are, Lucy.'

Lucy nearly stayed where she was; just one foot went out of the bathroom and tried to walk downstairs by itself. She imagined it going off alone into the garden, joined to her by a long leg. 'We only came to tell Robin about . . .' she began to say, but Biddy stopped her.

'I'll tell,' she said. 'I saw it first.'

'I knew what it was first,' said Lucy.

'I liked it best,' said Kate. 'So I should tell.'

'It was one of those steam engines,' said Biddy. 'That you told us about.'

'Up on the road,' said Lucy.

'Yes, of course,' said Mummy, not believing them at all. She pulled Robin out of the bath. 'I've had a steam engine in here too.'

'Ours was bigger than that,' said Kate. 'I think.'

'Really and truly,' said Biddy. 'Truly and truthly.'

'Honestly and golden,' said Kate.

'It was black,' said Lucy. 'It came along the road.'

'I want to see it,' said Robin. 'Take me out.'

But they told him it had gone now, on towards Oxford. Mummy thought they would see it the next day, perhaps. The girls told him just what it had been like. There had been two men in it, one of them turning a wheel to make it steer. There had been smoke coming from its big chimney, and a coaly-steamy smell, and one of the men had a poker, and the big wheels went round and round, and a small wheel at the top had gone quickest of all.

Robin got drier and drier, because Mummy was seeing to that, and crosser and crosser, because he

wanted to have seen the steam engine going along the road. When he was dry he trod on Kate, but she understood him and did not mind, and that made him more cross. He bit Lucy but not quite as hard as he meant. Lucy bit him. He tasted of Daddy's blue soap. He punched Biddy, and she picked him up and carried him to his bed. Mummy was busy getting Kate's clothes off. Kate was holding her hands together so that her clothes

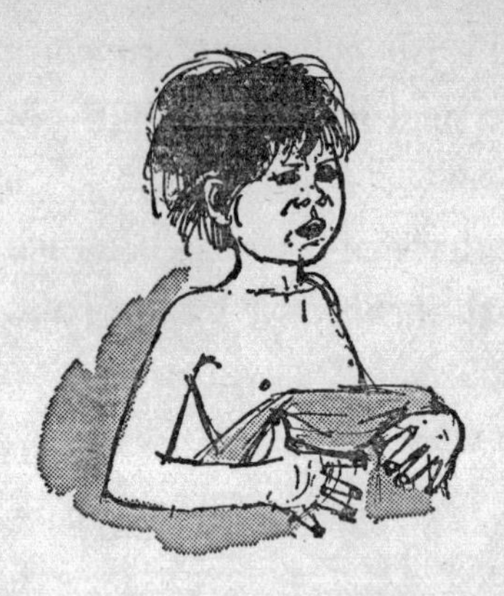

would not come off. Mummy picked her up and put her in the bath with all sorts of vests and dresses hung on her arms. Kate was very cross, and said the water was too hot and too cold and used.

'Bathtime,' said Mummy, 'is supposed to be a nice calm part of the day when a mother and her children can have pleasant splashy conversations and everything can be happy and gentle. But it's never like that. Lucy, come in here at once and get into that bath. Biddy, stop teasing Robin.'

Then there was a little more fuss because Biddy was not teasing Robin, but she was making him excited so that he wouldn't go to sleep. And Lucy had done what Mummy said and got into the bath at once, with her shoes and socks and all her clothes on.

'Robin and I are going downstairs, away from

you all,' said Mummy. 'So the longer you are in the bath the better. And you can stay in bed tomorrow, Lucy, you'll have nothing to wear.' She went downstairs with Robin and Daddy's blue soap.

Mummy was in the kitchen, but Robin was in the playroom when he heard the noise outside. He was thinking that it was no good being a steam engine if only the girls had seen one. If he had been a girl he would have come in and told Robin about it before it went away. He knew that. And it was no good being a steam engine if he was being the wrong colour or had the wrong lot of wheels.

He left the steam engine part of him in the middle of the playroom and went with the rest of him to the window and looked out. Outside there was the garden, and then there was the garden gate, and then there was part of a farmyard and then there was the lane that went up to the road. And just coming down the lane and into the farmyard there was a big black smoky thing with huge wheels, and it was going clank and whistle and slowly puff puff puff puff, and a man was turning a little wheel and another man was standing beside him pulling at a black lever and they were both riding on the black machine. Robin knew what it was. It was a steam engine, and it had come to visit him, because only the girls had seen it before, and it knew Robin ought to see it too.

Robin went straight outside. It was raining again, just a little bit, but he didn't care. He

walked across the garden and into the farmyard and watched. The steam engine came down the yard and stopped. Then it went backwards a little

way, and forwards again, and it had turned round. It went forward as far as the water pump and then it stopped again. It was nearly quiet when it stopped. There was just a little kettley noise and some kettley steam.

One of the men jumped down to the ground from the little place where he had stood. He undid part of the machine and looked inside it. Then he lifted a bucket from a hook at the back of the steam engine and began to fill it with water from the pump. Robin saw that there were all sorts of things hanging on the engine, like shovels and ropes and chains and boxes and baskets.

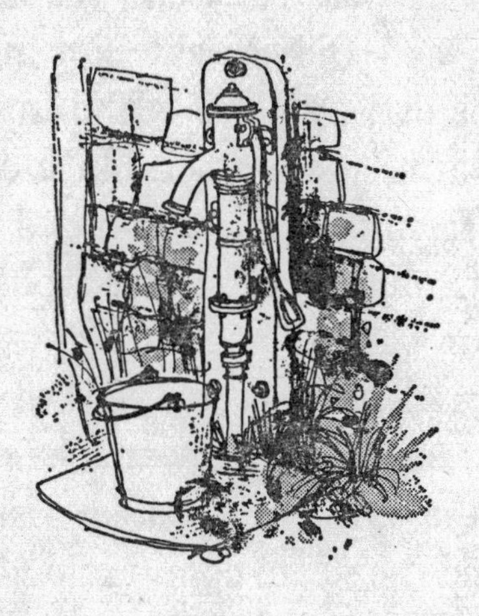

The man filled the bucket and Robin waited for him to start washing the engine. Daddy washed the car at that pump. But the man began to pour the water into the engine, into the place where he had looked. Robin knew that was wrong, and he ran across the yard to tell the man.

'That's not petrol,' he said. 'That's a water pump, because it hasn't got a light on it.'

'Ah,' said the man, 'but we don't use petrol. We don't use petrol, do we, Bill?' he said to the man up on the engine.

'We use coal,' said the man called Bill. 'Hand him up, Jack, and we'll show him how it goes.'

'Are you ready?' said the man with the bucket. Robin said he was ready and the man lifted him up to Bill, and Bill caught him and stood him down in the driving place of the engine.

It was warm, and it smelt like a coal wagon. It was warm from the fire. Bill opened the door, and the fire was much too hot for Robin's bare feet. All the floor was too hot for him really, so he sat on the edge of the coal and looked at the wheels and levers, and watched water being poured in, and saw the hot clear smoke rising from the chimney and the steam coming cloudy from different places.

Then there was enough water in the engine. The bucket went into its place, and the pump dribbled a bit on to its stone.

'Take her away,' said Jack.

'Start her up,' said Bill.

'Me?' said Robin. Bill said Yes, and told him which lever to pull. Robin pulled it. Nothing much happened for a moment, and then all the wheels and rods and joints moved at once, and Robin was driving a steam engine across the farmyard.

'We'll have to leave you,' said Bill. 'It's bed time, isn't it? But if you come to the fair to-morrow you'll see us working a roundabout.' He picked Robin up from his place in the coal and handed him down to Jack. Jack put him on the ground.

'Don't forget to come to see us,' he said. 'You'll

know the name of our roundabout by this,' and he put something into the little pocket of Robin's pyjama jacket. Then he ran after the steam engine and climbed up the back of it and into the driving place. Robin stood in the yard, feeling at his pocket, which had something soft and lumpy in it, and watched them go all the way up the lane and on to the road. Then he turned round and went into the house again.

The girls had finished their bath and were coming downstairs, flapping the wet ends of the long hair into each others' faces.

'Robin,' said Biddy. 'You've just been washed.'

'I'm clean,' said Robin. 'Mummy cleaned me.'

'Oh, Robin,' said Lucy. 'Come and show Mummy. Mummy, look at Robin; he's absolutely filthy again.'

'Don't tease,' said Mummy, from the kitchen.

'He couldn't help it,' said Kate. 'Could you, Robin? I expect it's all from the dirty floor.'

'Kate, you're being unkind to me,' said Mummy. 'I have clean floors.' Then she came out of the kitchen and saw Robin. 'Oh,' she said. 'Lucy, you were quite right. He's filthy. How did you get like that, Robin?'

They looked at him and counted up how dirty he was. He had great big black handmarks from Bill and Jack under his arms, where they had lifted him up and down. He had a black coaly patch where he had sat on the coal. He had dirty feet from walking in the wet yard. He had py-

jamas all dampened by rain. He had black hands from starting the engine. He had a black greasy mark on his face, and all sorts of smudges and touches everywhere.

'I was driving a steam engine,' he said. 'Out in the yard.'

'Come in again at once,' said Mummy. 'Biddy, Lucy, Kate, and even Robin.' But it was no good her saying anything. They had all gone out into the yard.

'Oh Robin,' said Kate. 'Where is it?'

'Gone to the fair,' said Robin. 'But there are its feetmarks.'

So they all looked at the big tracks the engine had left, where it had turned round. Then the girls nearly thought it was true, though Lucy thought Robin might have drawn them all with his toes, which would have made them dirty.

'It's gone to Oxford Fair,' said Robin. 'Read this, Biddy,' and he pulled out the thing the man had put in his pocket.

'It's a red balloon,' said Biddy. 'Do people read balloons?'

'Blow it up,' said Lucy. 'It might speak.'

Biddy blew it up, and then she could read it, because there was writing on it, and drawing too. It said 'Faringdon and Gurney, Steam Traction Limited', and an address and a telephone number.

‘That’s it,’ said Robin. ‘They’ve drawn it. That’s Bill and that’s Jack, and that’s where I was.’

Mummy came out then, to catch Robin once more.

‘It’s a trick,’ said Lucy. ‘It must be a trick; it’s just you and Robin playing, isn’t it, Mummy? You did it while we had our bath.’

Robin had been looking up the lane and along the road, the way the engine had gone. ‘There,’ he said, and he pointed. Along the road, at the top of the hill, there was a lumpy thing going out of sight, with smoke coming from it.

‘It’s just smoke,’ said Biddy. ‘But I think it looks like a steam engine.’

‘I don’t,’ said Lucy.

‘I do,’ said Kate. ‘It’s all right, Robin, it’s just

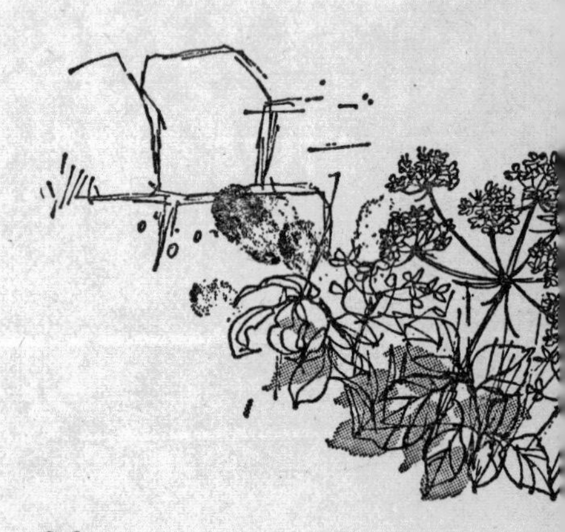

like one.' But Kate was looking in quite the wrong place and only being kind.

The black thing on the road sent up two lots of steam, and then it went behind the hedges.

'It was just like one,' said Mummy.

And then they all knew it had really been one,

because they heard the noise of whistles coming twice, and only steam engines make whistlings like that.

'It was true,' said Lucy. 'Robin's was true. But ours wasn't true; we didn't see one before.'

'No,' said Biddy.

'It was just your jolly fun,' said Mummy. 'Well I never.'

'It was really a man on a bicycle,' said Biddy. 'We changed him into something better for Robin.'

'Me?' said Robin. 'I'm going to stay dirty, like this. Steam engines are dirty. Steam engines are black. I want some coal for supper, that's what they eat.'

But they bathed him again, all the same, and gave him bread and butter.

The Big Egg

Illustrated by

Margery Gill

'Daddy, did you know I could read the table-cloth?' said Katharine.

'She can't really, it's just some sugar she's spilt,' said Adam. 'I've spilt some too. Mine says Adam.'

Ellen looked at Adam's sugar, and then she looked at Katharine's sugar. Then she looked at some crumbs that had fallen round her own plate. She moved them with her fingers, 'Mine says Bread,' she said.

'I will read them all,' said Daddy. 'Katharine's says, Go and wash the marmalade off your hands and off your chin. Adam's says, I must clean my shoes, and Ellen's says, Go up to the farm for the paper.'

'I thought it would say something like that,' said Ellen. 'Let me read your crumbs, Daddy.'

Daddy said he had read his. His crumbs said he was going to read his letters whilst Ellen went for the paper. Then he was going to read the paper.

Then he was going out into the Alder wood to chop a tree into pieces and bring it home.

Griselda was washing up at the sink. She said she would wash up for a long time, because there was a lot to do, and then cook for a long time, and then it would be lunch time. After that, if every-

body was good, they could go on a picnic, and leave Daddy to get on with some of his work. Daddy was writing a book. He kept writing books.

A train went rumbling by on the electric line.

'Twenty past nine,' said Daddy. He knew all the trains. Ellen often thought he could have been an engine driver and taken them all for long train rides. They could all sit with him at the front of the train and see everything. They could keep going past their own house, and look down at it. They would have to look down, because the trains ran by high up on a bank.

Adam thought that someone might come to play today. 'Did it rain?' he said. If it had rained the road to the house was so muddy that people didn't like to come.

'It didn't rain,' said Daddy. 'Katharine still has marmalade on her chin. I shall read your crumbs again.'

'Griselda makes very sticky marmalade,' said Katharine. 'It isn't my chin sticking to the marma-

lade, it's the marmalade sticking to my chin.'

'Come on, dabble,' said Griselda. She meant, Wash.

'Yes, Griselda,' said Katharine.

Adam put on his Wellington boots. It was summer time, and it hadn't rained, but the road could be muddy any time. He put his boots on, and then he cleaned his shoes. Ellen put her boots on too. Katharine dried her chin, and put hers on.

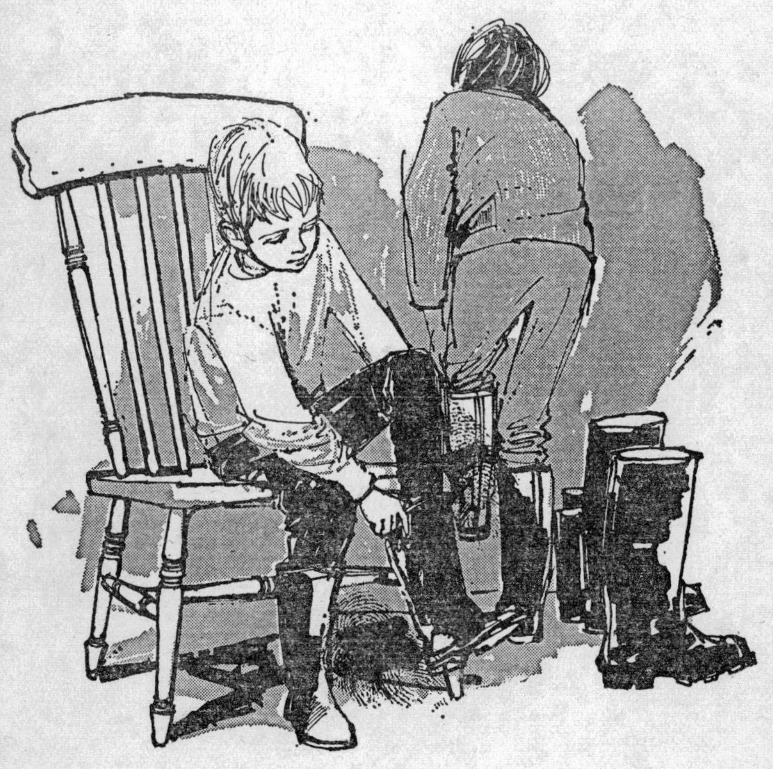

‘We’re all going,’ said Adam.

Outside there was sunshine in the apple trees, and sunshine on the wires over the railway. They were the wires that the train got its electricity from. Another train came along the line, and the wire shook. The train wore a thing on its head like horns, and that touched the wire.

There was a cow looking over the gate. She was

wanting to eat the garden. Ellen stayed on the garden side of the gate until the cow got tired of looking and went away.

'If you look at a cow for a long time it goes away,' said Adam. 'I think it does.'

'I think it goes away even if you don't look at it,' said Ellen.

'I think it looks back at you,' said Katharine 'Then I go away, if it does that.'

The cow went away and they could hear it tearing up grass and see it swallowing it.

The road was muddy at the sides, where car wheels kept squashing it, and grassy in the middle. They walked on the grass. They crossed the field, and came down to the bridge over the stream. The road was more cindery and dry here, and they did not have to walk only in the middle.

Adam looked back at the house. The cow was looking over the gate again. He stared at the cow, but it did not go away.

'I'm too far off,' he said. Ellen and Katharine helped him to look. The cow took no notice at all.

'It is too far off,' said Katharine. 'Even me, I'm not going away.'

They went up towards the farm. The road went between high banks now. Adam thought it would be a good idea to climb one of the banks. Ellen thought it would be a good idea to stay in the road. Katharine thought it would be a good idea to climb the other bank, and get into the hedge. So she did. They went up the hill like that, and there was the farm in front of them.

Adam came down the bank, to Ellen. They waited for Katharine. Katharine did not come. They called for her, and still she didn't come.

'Perhaps she walked the wrong way,' said Adam. 'When she got to the top of the bank she didn't know which way to turn. She would be nearly home now.'

'If she did go nearly home, she would look at the cow, and the cow would look back, and she would come here again,' said Ellen.

'I'll find her,' said Adam, and he got into the hedge at the top of the bank, and walked along inside it.

It was not very easy to walk in the hedge. It was a wide hedge, and it was more like being in a little

wood than being in a hedge. Trees grew up in it, and prickly brambles, and thorny roses, and nettles. But there was always a way through, because there were little pathways everywhere.

He walked along. Then he saw Katharine. She

was lying on the ground, curled up. She looked at him, and said, 'Hush.'

'Why?' said Adam, not hushing at all, but talking in his ordinary voice.

'I'm hatching,' said Katharine.

'You hatched a long time ago,' said Adam, 'about six years ago. And you were born, you weren't hatched.'

Ellen had walked along the road. She couldn't see Adam, she couldn't see Katharine. But she could hear their voices.

'What are you doing?' she called.

'Tell her quietly,' said Katharine.

Adam went out of the hedge, on to the bank,

and looked down. 'She says she's hatching,' he said.

Ellen came up to see. She saw Katharine lying in the hedge.

'Get up at once,' she said. 'It's all damp and you'll spoil your clothes.'

'Do be quiet, Ellen,' said Katharine. 'I'm hatching this egg.'

And she showed them what she was curled round. It was an egg. It was a big blue egg, much bigger than a hen's egg. It was blue, but it had speckles on it as well.

'Where did you find that?' said Ellen. 'Is it real?'

'I laid it,' said Katharine. 'I felt funny, so I

curled up, and there was the egg. I think it's going to hatch.'

'Oh, Katharine,' said Ellen, 'they take weeks and weeks to hatch.'

'I shall stay here for weeks and weeks,' said Katharine. 'You can come back after lunch and see.'

'Weeks are longer than that,' said Ellen. 'And

I'm sure you didn't lay it. People don't lay eggs, and you haven't any feathers.'

'They're growing,' said Katharine.

Ellen picked up the egg. She had never seen such a big one. It was warm, much warmer than Katharine could have made it. It was heavy.

'It might be an eagle's egg,' said Adam, looking up at the sky. 'I shall look at the eagle, and it will go away.'

Katharine was going to cry. She uncurled herself and sat up. She cried best when she was sitting up.

'It's all right,' said Ellen, 'we'll take it home. It'll hatch better there. And it isn't an eagle's egg. It's a, well, I don't know what make it is.'

'It's a Katharine egg,' said Katharine. 'A Katharine egg. I laid it.'

'We'll take it home and show Griselda,' said Ellen. 'Daddy wants the paper to read. And you can sit on a cushion at home, and hatch it there.'

'There'll be a baby Katharine inside it,' said Katharine. 'Another of me, but it'll be mine.'

'It'll have feathers,' said Adam.

Katharine came out of the hedge, and down on to the road. 'You carry it,' she said. 'If I want one I'll lay it.'

They went to the farm for the paper. The paper was delivered there, and the farmer left it in the porch of the house, ready for them to pick up. Adam picked it up.

Ellen carried the egg, Adam carried the paper, and Katharine found a leaf with a hole in it, and carried that.

As they were coming out of the gate of the farm they met the farmer. 'Hello,' he said. 'What have you got there?'

'A leaf,' said Katharine.

'The paper,' said Adam.

'The egg Katharine laid,' said Ellen.

'Did she now,' said the farmer. 'That's a tale, Katharine.'

'I laid it in a hedge,' said Katharine. 'I felt funny, and laid it, and we're taking it home to hatch it on a cushion. There's another me inside.'

'You never laid that,' said the farmer. 'That's a turkey egg. It was laid by a turkey. All you'll get out of that is egg meat.'

'I felt as if I'd laid it,' said Katharine.

'One of my turkeys laid it,' said the farmer. 'A little lass like you would never lay a big blue egg like that.'

Ellen took the egg to him. 'It's yours,' she said. 'Where shall I put it?'

'Oh,' said Adam. 'But we found it.'

'I found it,' said Katharine. 'I laid it.'

'Well,' said the farmer, 'if I'd never seen it I would never have missed it, would I? And I wouldn't have looked in the hedge.' He picked the egg up. 'It's warm,' he said. 'It hasn't been laid so long.'

'Just now,' said Katharine.

'Hush,' said Ellen. 'We're tired of that story.'

'So am I,' said Katharine. 'It was just lying there, and I felt funny, so I had to hatch it.'

The farmer handed the egg back to Ellen. She took it in two hands.

'You might as well have it,' he said. 'But you can hatch it from now to Christmas, and it'll never turn into turkey, or into anything. It'll never hatch. But it's fresh, and the best thing you can do is eat it.'

'I'll have it for my tea,' said Katharine.

'You can have it for all your teas, I shouldn't wonder,' said the farmer. 'There's more there than you'll eat.'

'Katharine has to say thank you,' said Adam. 'Hasn't she?'

'We all have,' said Ellen; so they all did.

They got the egg home safely, taking it in turns to carry it, and taking turns to carry the newspaper and the leaf with a hole in it.

When they got home they stared at the cow until she went away, because she was still looking over the gate. They went in, and made a nest in the grass at the foot of an apple tree, and put the egg in the nest. Adam went to fetch Daddy and Griselda. He would not tell them why they had to come. Ellen and Katharine stayed behind to watch the egg.

'It hasn't moved,' said Katharine, when she saw Daddy and Griselda coming.

'What have you found?' said Griselda. 'I hope it's nothing dangerous.'

Then she saw what it was. 'Isn't it pretty,' she said. 'What is it?'

'Katharine said she laid it,' said Adam.

'I said it once,' said Katharine. 'I felt as if I'd laid it.'

'It looks like a piece of sky that's been in the mud,' said Daddy. 'Blue and speckly. Who did lay it, if it wasn't Katharine?'

'I think it was me,' said Katharine.

'A turkey laid it,' said Ellen. 'Katharine wanted to hatch it, but at the farm they told us it would never hatch. Inside it's just an ordinary egg, but big. Outside it's like that. It's new-laid. It was quite hot when Katharine found it.'

'I like it,' said Daddy. 'May I pick it up?'

They let him pick it up. He took it indoors, and put it on the table, and looked at it.

'What are you going to do with it?' said Griselda. 'Keep it?'

‘Eat it,’ said Katharine. ‘For tea.’

Daddy thought it would be a pity to break the shell; but Katharine had stopped being the mother of an egg now. She was hoping to eat it. Daddy knew what to do.

‘I don’t want to smash the shell,’ he said. ‘So I’ll get the inside out kindly. I’ll cut the egg right round the middle, with a saw, and Griselda can scramble the inside, and we can keep the two pieces of shell.’

'They can go on the shelf near the plates,' said Ellen. 'They can be cups for visitors.'

Daddy drew a careful pencil line round the waist of the egg. Then he got his little saw and held it between his knees, with the teeth up. And instead of sawing the egg as if it were a piece of wood, he rubbed the egg-shell gently against the saw, all along the pencil mark.

Gradually, instead of the black pencil mark there was a white saw mark. Underneath the blue outside there was a white shell.

The mark gradually came round the egg. There was an inch of pencil mark, then half an inch, then quarter of an inch, then nothing.

'I shall have to go round again,' said Daddy. 'It isn't ready to break yet.'

Griselda thought of something they needed. 'A good thing you've got a housewife,' she said; and she brought a basin to put the inside of the egg in. Ellen held the basin.

Daddy began to go round the second time. White powder from the shell fell on to his knees.

Then he held the egg in two hands over the basin, and gave a little twist. Nothing happened.

'It isn't ready yet,' he said. He had to put it on the saw again. 'I'm getting to know the marks on it,' he said. 'I hope they were right at the farm, and it's a good egg. I don't think I would like a rotten egg to break on to my knees.'

The egg did not break on his knees. He held it over the basin again, and twisted with both hands. The egg suddenly broke in two, and the inside slithered out. There was a great deal of white of

egg, all runny, and there was a great big yolk. They ran into the basin, and looked at everybody like a huge eye.

'It's staring,' said Katharine. Griselda took the basin away, ready to cook the egg.

Daddy looked at the two half shells in his hand. They were like two cups. One was round at the bottom, and the other was thin, and they were as thick as the best cups in the world, which is quite thick for egg shells, but very thin for cups.

He rinsed them at the sink, and put them at the back of the stove to dry. Then he put the saw away. Then he settled down to read the paper.

After lunch Griselda did a little more cooking. She took the egg and stirred it up, so that it was no longer an eye looking out of the basin, but a yellow mixture. She put in salt and pepper and butter,

poured it all into a pan, put it on the stove, and stirred for a long time.

At the end of the long time there was scrambled egg, and a lot of it, too. Griselda put it to cool. No one would want to eat just yet.

When the turkey's egg was cool Griselda mixed in some salad dressing, and made sandwiches. They were sandwiches for the picnic. There were other things as well, but the egg sandwiches were the most important. She packed some in a bag, and left some out for Daddy, who was beginning

to get to his table and write. He would find it easier to work in a quiet house.

Then Griselda took Ellen and Adam and Katharine, and the sandwiches, out for the picnic.

They walked along the side of the railway, in the field, and the trains went rumbling by, and had to be waved to.

They went under the bridge, and out into the far wood, and had tea under a tree.

Katharine looked at her first sandwich. 'I shall say hello to the sandwich,' she said. 'I was going to hatch you, sandwich, and you were going to be

another me. The naughty one, so that I didn't get into trouble any more.'

'It'll be you,' said Griselda. 'That sandwich will turn into you, the same old naughty you. So bite it and see.'

Katharine bit it.

'I do taste nice,' she said.

Adam had eaten two sandwiches already. He looked at the crumbs he had dropped.

'I shall eat some more,' he said. 'I can't quite read what the crumbs say yet.'

Ellen looked at his crumbs. 'You'll have to hurry,' she said. 'The ants are coming to take the crumbs away. They'll rub out all the words before you know what they say.'

'Last time I had to clean my shoes,' said Adam 'So perhaps I don't mind if I never find out what the crumbs say this time.'

'Another sandwich, please Griselda,' said Katharine.

And there, in the wood, they finished all the big blue egg that Katharine had found in the hedge. And what they didn't finish the ants took away the same night.

The Toffee Join

Illustrated by
Shirley Hughes

'It's raining,' said Diana. She huffed her breath on to the window and drew on the steamy mark with her finger. She drew a smile and a nose and two eyes, but before she could draw the chin and the hair and the ears the mark had gone away.

'It's been raining all day,' said Mother. 'That's why I'm sitting quietly at home doing some darning. That's why your brother wants to go out and play in the garden. He always goes by contraries.'

'Granny said,' said Diana, 'that next time it was raining and we hadn't anything to do, she would like me to take her half a pound of treacle.'

'Yes,' said Mother, 'that would be a good idea. But before you do that you'd better go to Michael's house, and then to Mervyn and Susan's house, and see whether they have to take anything on the next wet day when they've got nothing to do.'

'Why would they want to go there?' said Diana.

'Why,' said Mother, 'she's Granny to all of you, isn't she? You put your coat on and ask Michael whether he wants to go, and then ask the other two as well.'

Diana came down from the window. 'I shall forget what I've gone for,' she said. 'They're all bigger than me. Can't we send Robin? Isn't that what brothers are for?'

But Mother thought that Diana could manage; and she helped her on with her coat, and opened the door, and pulled up her hood, and sent her off.

'I shall watch you,' said Mother. 'I can see your red coat from a long way off.'

Diana went down the path, out of the gate, and along the side of the road close to the wall. In the village where she lived there was no pavement, so everybody had to walk in the road.

Michael's house was nearly next door, and Michael was lying by the fire scuffing the carpet up with his boots.

'What do *you* want?' he said. He did not think Diana was the sort of visitor you have to be polite to. Diana explained that it was a wet day and there was nothing to do, and that Granny wanted half a pound of treacle.

'What about it, then?' said Michael.

'We're going to take her some,' said Diana. 'Me and Robin. Mother thought you might want to go.'

'No. I'm all right here,' said Michael. But his mother, who was sister to Diana's mother, came through from her kitchen and said: 'Yes, you do want to go to Granny's, because she said that next time it rained and I couldn't keep you from scuffing up the carpet with your boots, you had to go up there and take her four ounces of butter. So I'll just get that ready, and then you can be off with Diana and her treacle.'

Michael got up from the fireside. 'Oh well,' he

said. 'If they all want looking after, then I suppose I'd better go.' And he let his face go into a way that meant he did a lot for other people and never got thanked; but putting his face like that made his chin tickle itself, and he ended up by laughing.

Diana said she would go and get the other two, the other cousins with the same Granny, Mervyn and Susan.

Mervyn and Susan had something to do already. They were putting together a big jig-saw puzzle. All they had was the edge, so that it looked like a picture that had been rubbed out; though it was really a picture that had not been rubbed in yet.

'Can I lay some?' said Diana; and she put in a piece that seemed to fit, and she wondered why Mervyn or Susan had not done it before.

'That's wrong,' said Susan. 'I'm sorry to say, my dear girl.' That was the way she sometimes talked. She got it from going to school and being in the middle class. All the other cousins were in the bottom class, except Diana, and she was in no class at all.

Mervyn and Susan's mother asked Diana why she had come out on such a wet day. Diana told her that they could all go to Granny's, because Granny wanted some treacle and some butter.

'Oh yes,' said Susan. 'And one day she wants half a pound of sugar, she said.'

'I remember,' said Susan's mother. 'And I think today would be a good day for you to take it.' So they weighed out half a pound of sugar and poured it into a bag, and turned the top of the bag over like the end of a sleeve that is too long. Mervyn put on his duffle coat with the wooden pegs instead of buttons, and put the sugar in his pocket. Susan put on her orange raincoat, and her mother

blinked at her and Diana, because one of them was red and the other one was orange.

'You do clash,' she said.

Michael was ready at his house. The butter was in a piece of greaseproof paper, in his anorak pocket. It had to be pushed back in now and then in case it fell out. 'I wasn't bringing any basket,' he said. 'I don't want to be messing on with baskets.'

They went to Diana's house, and stood in a row in the kitchen.

'What a lot of us,' said Mother, putting them all in order of height and age. Tallest was Susan, then Michael, then Mervyn, then Robin, and then Diana. Robin was the fat one.

'Just what to put the treacle in,' said Mother. 'I know, I'll put it in a plastic bag, and that'll be easy to carry, and hard to break, and the rain won't get into it. If some clever fingers will hold the bag open I'll pour the treacle in.'

There were five clever fingers, one from each person, so that the bag was held very wide open while Mother spooned in half a jar of golden syrup. It sat all smiling in the clear plastic. Robin, of course, let go of his piece of the bag when he wriggled his holding finger straight and got a nailful of treacle. He licked it off when the job was

done. Mother twisted the neck of the bag round on itself and tied a knot, and gave the bag to Diana to carry. She said that Robin would be untwisting it and getting his fingers in.

'*I* won't,' said Diana. 'I'm good.' She was good until Mother knelt down in front of her to pull her socks to her knees for her. Then Diana sat the golden bagful on the back of Mother's neck.

'Oh, it does feel funny,' said Mother, rubbing the back of her neck to see whether any treacle had got out on to it. None had. All the others had to have the cold clingy bag on the backs of their necks too. Then Mother said they were ready to go, and sent them out of the door and down the garden and over the stile into the field. In the field there was a path made of big flat flagstones, and

they walked along it in a line, with Diana in front, and Susan at the back.

'We look after the boys,' said Diana. 'We're mothers.'

'I'd rather have the cat,' said Michael; but the other two did not mind at all.

The path led them across the field and to another wall with a stile in it. It was a high wall, and there were some steps up to it, and down the other side. Here they met a dog they knew called Rover. He was waiting for his master, who was working in a barn close by. Rover stood in the middle of the stile, and he would not get out of the way for Diana.

'Out of the way, good boy,' said Diana, pushing at him with one hand. In the other hand was the bag of treacle. But Rover stood at the top of the steps and looked down at her, and wagged his tail slowly, and looked right over Diana's head at the far distance.

Robin came next, with his hands tight in his pockets so that he looked fatter than ever. Rover looked at him, and gave him a nudge with his nose, so that Robin fell down in the rain off the steps, and rolled in the grass. He got up still

smiling, because he nearly always smiled, and waited to see how the other two boys managed. Mervyn was next, and he had a pull at Rover's collar, but Rover hunched his shoulders and would not come. Then Michael tried to push Rover, and Rover seemed to think Michael was stronger, and he went backwards down the steps the other side of the stile. It was hard work for Michael, because he had to put one arm round Rover's neck and heave and heave. But at last Rover was out of the

way, and they all went through the stile. Rover sat down in the lane, and began to undo some paper he had found, and lick what was inside.

Michael found what it was when he looked in

his pocket. Rover had taken the butter from the pocket, and that was what he had unwrapped. When Michael ran back to him, Rover had finished the butter and left the paper. He gave Michael a buttery kiss on the cheek, and went back to watching the stile.

'Never mind,' said Susan. 'It'll give him a bad pain, and then he'll be sorry; and we'll tell Granny, and she won't mind if you haven't brought any butter.'

'We can have jam and bread without butter,' said Diana.

Michael picked up the empty paper, and put that in his pocket, just to show Granny when they got there. Then they all ran down the lane. They were careful to run in the middle of it, because it was a muddy lane where tractors came, and along

both sides there were muddy ruts full of water. Along the middle there was grass.

Then they ran on to a hard flat piece of lane, where somebody had made the ground firm with stones.

They were slippery stones. First Mervyn skidded

and rolled over, and then Robin, who rolled much further. Then Diana was next. She skidded on the stones and sat down.

Michael and Susan stopped running before they

came to the slippery part. Susan came to help Diana get up.

'Did you hurt yourself?' said Susan.

'No,' said Diana. 'Isn't it funny, it was quite soft.'

'Good,' said Susan; and she went to pick the boys up, and left Diana to get up on her own. They all got up, and found that no one was hurt;

and they ran on again. Granny's house was beyond the end of the lane, through another field, and they were nearly there.

Diana found she was not carrying the treacle any more. She had dropped it. She thought it was a good thing it had not been in a glass jar, or in a tin the lid could fall from. She looked round, and found the bag, sitting on the stony ground like a blister. She picked it up and ran on with the others.

She went past Susan and Michael and Robin, and she was just going to run past Mervyn when Susan called to her to stop, because the treacle was getting out.

Diana stopped, and looked at the treacle. One of the corners of the bag had split, and the golden stuff was running slowly out and leaving a trail on the grass of the lane.

'Stop it running out,' said Susan. But they did

not know how to stop it running. Diana put her finger against it, but the treacle ran round her finger, and she had to suck it dry. Mervyn thought a leaf might do it, if he pressed it on firmly. But the leaf fell off with the treacle. Michael thought Diana should hold the bag upside-down, but that was too difficult to do.

'Then we'll just hurry,' said Susan. 'And get there before it all runs out. Quick, run.'

So they ran again, through the gate at the end of the lane, and across the field, where there was only a track, and through another gate into the rest of the lane, and there was Granny's house.

They all ran up to the door, and they all banged on it. Even Robin banged with his head. He had taken one hand from his pocket, but he was using that to catch the trailing treacle, a fingerful at a time.

Granny came to the door, and there was such a noise when she did, because everybody spoke at once. She had to tell them all to be quiet, and then make Susan say what they all wanted.

'A plate,' said Susan, 'please Granny, very quickly.'

Granny brought a plate very quickly, and Diana lifted up the treacle bag and laid it on the plate.

But they were too late. The treacle had finished running out. Instead of a full, fat, golden bag there was a thin, wrinkled, empty one, with a few drops of gold here and there. And that was all.

‘Oh dear,’ said Granny. ‘It does look out of breath, doesn’t it? What happened?’

Susan explained how nearly all of them had fallen down, and the treacle bag had fallen too. Then she told Granny how they had met Rover, and Rover had eaten the butter he had taken from Michael’s pocket.

‘But is the sugar safe?’ said Granny. ‘That will be something.’

‘Of course it is,’ said Mervyn, patting his pocket. He put his hand in, and pulled out the paper bag and held it up to Granny. But all the sugar stayed in his pocket, because the bottom had come out of the bag.

He took off his coat, and Granny tipped his pocket out. There was half a pound of sugar, a toffee paper, a piece of chewing-gum, a length of string, two hazel nuts, a tooth from his own

mouth, and a tooth he had picked up in a field, an apple core not quite eaten down to the middle yet, a bendy potato crisp, and two stones tied together with wire, part of an invention. There was a lot of grimy dust as well. And the sugar had turned damp, and turned grey too.

'Well,' said Granny, 'you haven't brought me any of the things I asked for, have you? But you needn't be sad about it, because it was no one's fault, was it?'

'It was naughty Rover, and the slippery stones, and just the oldness of the bag,' said Susan. 'They couldn't help that, could they, all these little ones?'

'No, they couldn't,' said Granny. 'And we old ones, that's you and me, Susan, will get some more sugar and treacle and butter from the cupboard and start from the beginning. And all the little ones can take off their wet things and hang them up to dry. And you'll all have to sit on the floor to take your boots and shoes off.'

It was a stone floor, but there were sacks on it, because the day was so wet, to stop wet footprints. They all sat on the sacks and took off their shoes and boots. Diana sat on one with a red diamond on it, and took off her shoes. She undid the laces.

Robin pulled off his boots. He had to use both his fat little hands.

When Diana stood up, the sack stood up with her. It had stuck to the back of her knees. Granny said: 'What are you doing, bairn?'

'The floor has got up with me,' said Diana. Granny came and pulled the sack away.

'No wonder,' said Granny. 'You know where

all that treacle went? It's all over the back of your knees. How did you manage that?'

'I know,' said Susan. 'She said the ground wasn't very hard when she slipped and sat down. She must have sat on the treacle bag, and that's what burst it.'

So Granny stopped weighing half a pound of

sugar, and stood Diana in the sink instead, with her socks on, and washed the socks and the treacle off together. Then she dried Diana's legs very briskly, and hung the wet socks by the stove to dry by themselves. Diana wished she was a sock, because it seemed to have an easier life.

'Now we can get on with the Toffee Join,' said Granny, drying her hands and beginning to pour treacle from a tin on to the weighed sugar. 'A Toffee Join is when people bring things to have them made into toffee, and when they've made the toffee they eat it,' she said. 'You all brought things, and I was going to make it with my pan and my stove. But now we'll make it with all my things, and share it out in the old-fashioned way, the same as my grandmother used to when I was a girl.'

The butter went into the pan first, and cracked itself smooth and hot. Then the sugar and the syrup went in on top of that, and the pan went quiet again.

Granny stirred and stirred with a wooden spoon. She said that no one must come too near, because toffee was hotter than the hottest water in the hottest kettle. She sent Susan to get a saucer of water, and stood that on the table. Robin wanted to know why it wasn't a saucer of milk. Granny said it was so that she could see to the bottom of the saucer, and no one could see through milk. The cat jumped on the table and looked into the saucer, and thought it was empty, and went down again.

'Not for you, puss,' said Granny. It was for testing the toffee. The toffee had begun to bubble in the pan, and a quick steam was coming from it. Granny picked some of the hot melted toffee up in

the spoon and poured it into the water. They all looked into the saucer. The toffee squirmed, and then stood still. Granny picked it up in her fingers.

It was warm, she said. Then she squeezed it, and then she ate it. 'My first taste,' she said. 'Not quite ready yet.'

The next time she tried it, it was ready. She told all five of them to stand by the table, while she walked across the kitchen with the pan. She told them to look out of the window and not watch her, because what happened next was the surprise part of a Toffee Join.

At the end of her kitchen was a very big stone slab, like a table with one edge built into the wall.

Usually it was covered with things like bread bins and crockery. Today it was empty, and that was where Granny went.

They could hear her pouring and scraping, and then they heard her put the pan down. Robin kept trying to turn himself round to have a look, and Diana kept turning him back.

'Don't look yet,' said Granny; and they heard her doing something with a knife. Then, when she had finished that she sent them all through into her sitting-room. There was no toffee there, but tea was all ready by the fire. So they had tea. Then, when they had finished tea Granny went into the kitchen again, saying that the Toffee Join was nearly ready. And then she called them through.

Now there was a white cloth spread on the big stone, with one edge folded back very neatly like a bed. And like little people asleep in the bed were five ends of toffee bars, lying on the stone, because at a Toffee Join the toffee is always spread on a stone slab in strips, with just the ends left showing, and each person chooses a piece, so that some get long pieces and some get short ones. No one can tell what is under the cloth and out of sight.

'Youngest first, this time,' said Granny. 'Diana.'

'This one,' said Diana, pointing.

'Put your finger on it,' said Granny. And when each person came up to choose, they were told to put a finger on what they had chosen. When they had finished Granny turned the cloth back. They saw that Robin had the longest piece, and Diana a middle-sized piece, and poor Susan had the shortest piece of all. Some people looked pleased, like Robin, and some looked sad, like Susan.

'I knew it would be like that,' said Granny, and she pulled the cloth right back, and there was another piece for each person, arranged so that the person with the longest piece now would get a short one later, and the person with the shortest piece now would get the longest later. So that everybody was pleased.

'Well, look at that,' said Granny, when she had got a knife and was going to lift the toffee from its place. They all looked, and they saw that the naughty cat had walked right across the toffee and left its footprints on every bar.

'It didn't touch the toffee,' said Granny. 'It walked across the cloth I put on top. Look, there are its footprints.'

There were ten bars of toffee, and there was a big puddle of it next to the bars, where Granny had

poured all the rest. It was the biggest share, she said. Then she said, 'What a funny shape it has on its top. Why, I do believe that bad cat has walked across all the toffee bars and curled up on the biggest piece of all and gone to sleep.'

'You can see where its elbows were,' said Susan.

'It would be nice and warm to lie on,' said Granny. 'And soft as well. It's a good thing there was a cloth on it, or the cat would have stuck down worse than Diana did. And cats are very bad to wash. They don't like it.'

'I know what you can do, Granny,' said Susan. 'You can cut up the cat shape, and it can be a sort of toffee jig-saw puzzle, pussy-cat shape.'

So Granny cut it up, and they muddled it up, and put it together, and then put it in three little paper bags, and took it home to eat the next day.

'And on another wet day,' said Granny, 'we'll have another Toffee Join.'

Also in Young Puffins

Bad Boys

ed. Eileen Colwell

Twelve splendid stories about naughty boys, by favourite authors like Helen Cresswell, Charlotte Hough, Barbara Softly and Ursula Moray Williams.

Duggie the Digger and His Friends

Michael Prescott

As well as Duggie the Digger, there are tales about Horace the Helicopter, Bertram the Bus and Vernon the Vacuum Cleaner. It will please little boys who are interested in mechanical things.

The Invisible Womble and Other Stories

Elisabeth Beresford

These five stories are retellings of some of the television adventures and reveal the Wombles at their funniest and best. This book will certainly ensure their place in the family long after they have left the studios and bolted the door of their burrow behind them.

The Bears on Hemlock Mountain

Alice Dalgliesh

'OF COURSE THERE ARE NO BEARS ON HEMLOCK MOUNTAIN,' said Jonathan to himself as he walked over the hill, but he was still afraid there might be!

Tales from the End Cottage
More Tales from the End Cottage

Eileen Bell

Two tabby cats and a peke live with Mrs Apple in a Northamptonshire cottage. They quarrel, have adventures and entertain dangerous strangers. A new author with a special talent for writing about animals. For reading aloud to 5 and over, private reading 7 plus.

Tales of Olga da Polga
Olga Meets Her Match
Olga Carries On

Michael Bond

Michael Bond's latest heroine is an enchantingly independent guinea-pig with a zest for adventure.

Something to Do

Septima

This Young Puffin Original gives suggestions for games to play and things to make and do each month, from January to December. It is designed to help mothers with young children at home.

Something to Make

Felicia Law

A varied and practical collection of things for children to make from odds and ends around the house, with very little extra outlay, by an experienced teacher of art and handicrafts. For children of 6 up.